Written by Kit Frost.
Illustrations by Steve James, Chris Dickason and Emiliano Migliardo.
Cover artwork based on designs by Thy Bui.

First published in Great Britain in 2026 by Red Shed, part of Farshore

An imprint of HarperCollins*Publishers*
1 London Bridge Street, London SE1 9GF
www.farshore.co.uk

HarperCollins*Publishers*
Macken House, 39/40 Mayor Street Upper, Dublin 1, D01 C9W8, Ireland

Red Shed is a registered trademark of HarperCollins*Publishers* Ltd.

978 0 00 883885 0
Printed and bound in the UK using 100% Renewable Electricity at CPI Group (UK) Ltd.
1

A CIP catalogue record for this title is available from the British Library.

Stay safe online. Any website addresses listed in this book are correct at the time of going to print. However, Farshore is not responsible for content hosted by third parties. Please be aware that online content can be subject to change and websites can contain content that is unsuitable for children. We advise that all children are supervised when using the internet.

FSC
www.fsc.org
MIX
Paper | Supporting responsible forestry
FSC® C013604

AMAZING JOKES FOR EVERY 9 YEAR OLD

RED SHED

Whether you love animals, science or sport, you'll find LOADS of hilarious jokes in this book to make you laugh your head off . . .

What do you call a unicorn's fart?

Why didn't the teddy bear eat its lunch?

What makes more noise than a T. rex?

Read on to find out the answers – and get ready to giggle.

What did the violin-playing orca do?

She joined the orca-stra.

Why was the driver happy when he left the tyre shop?

He'd got a wheely good deal.

Which animal can hit an apple the furthest?

A fruit bat.

Can a frog jump higher than the Eiffel Tower?

Yes – buildings can't jump.

What did the polar bear put in its salad?

Iceberg lettuce.

What did the four-sided shape have for lunch?

A square meal.

Why do ducks always get parts in plays?

Because they are great quack-tors.

Why was the computer poorly?

It had a virus.

Knock, knock.

Who's there?

Would.

Would who?

Would-n't you like to know?

Did you hear about the swede that was always late?

It would never turnip on time.

What's big, grey and can't climb trees?

A castle.

Two goldfish were talking together in their tank. One goldfish said to the other goldfish, 'Do you know how to drive this?'

Did you hear about peanut butter's secret?

Don't spread it around.

Did you hear about the swimmer who got into big trouble?

He was in at the deep end.

Did you hear about the river that lost its current?

It was searching high and flow.

Where do horses go when they are ill?

The horse-pital.

What did the cheese say to its friend?

What did the cheese say when it was late?

I'd feta get going.

Why did the Olympic sprinter get kicked out of the music shop?

Because she was a record breaker.

How do you turn a bath into a bubble bath?

Eat lots of beans.

What do you call a unicorn's fart?

A rainbow.

How much does a rainbow weigh?

Not a lot – they are pretty light.

Why was the painter so smelly?

He was leading a fart class.

Why was the cow bored of jokes?

She had herd them all.

Why did the nose stop putting up its hand in lessons?

It always got picked anyway.

Knock, knock.

Who's there?

How are.

How are who?

I'm fine, thanks.

What did the egg say to its friends when they were late?

'We'd better get cracking.'

Why was the cow bad at driving?

Because she kept using the horn.

What's invisible and smells like fish?

A penguin's fart.

What is a cheese's favourite part of Christmas?

The Christmas crackers.

Knock, knock.

Who's there?

None-a.

None-a who?

None-a your business.

What did the chicken say to her friend before the start of the race?

'Good cluck.'

What's a scarecrow's favourite fruit?

Straw-berries.

Did you hear about the angry frog?

It was hopping mad.

Knock, knock.

Who's there?

Dinosaur.

Dinosaur who?

ROOOOOAAAAARR.

What did the annoyed plate of pasta say?

Why did the spaghetti cross the road?

Because it saw a fork coming up ahead.

What did the egg read for a laugh?

A yolk book.

What is an ice cream's favourite day of the week?

Sundae.

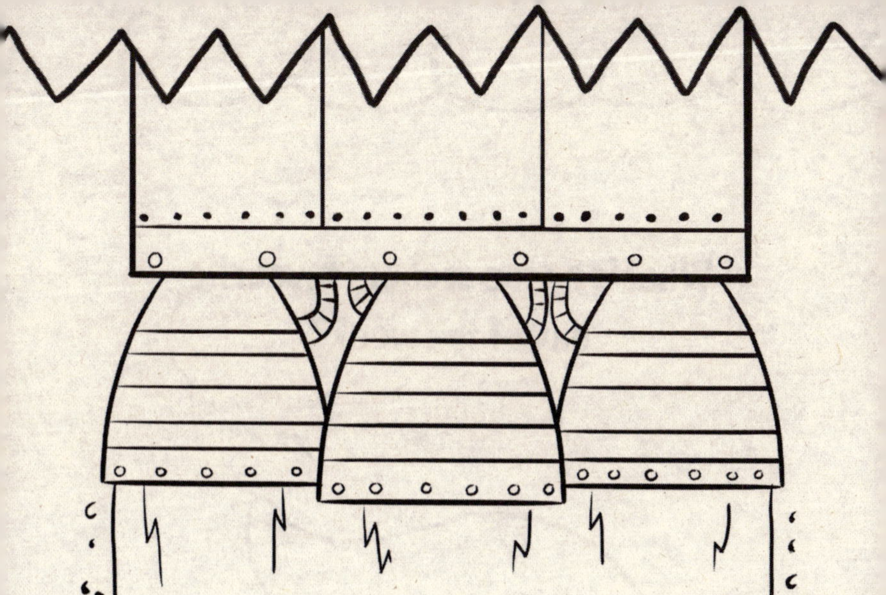

When do astronauts eat their sandwiches?

At launch time.

Why do polar bears never wear pants?

Because they've always got a bear bottom.

What sort of year is a frog's favourite?

A leap year.

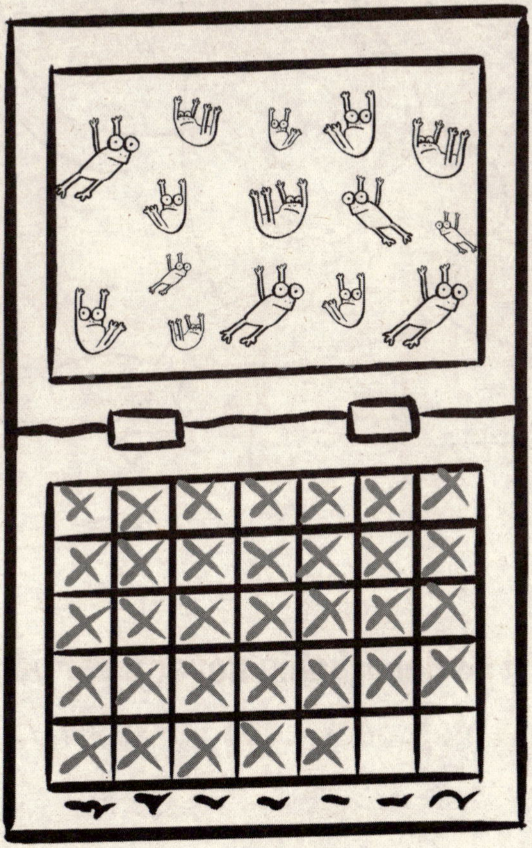

Why can you never hear a pterodactyl go to the toilet?

Because its pee is silent.

What do you call an ancient Roman with a cold?

Julius Sneeze-er.

Why was the mummy feeling stressed?

Because his little sister had wound him up.

How do Vikings send secret messages to each other?

They use Norse code.

What's an untidy archaeologist's favourite ancient civilization?

Messy-potamia.

Knock, knock.

Who's there?

Figs.

Figs who?

Figs the door knocker.

Why did the cat go to prison?

Because it had broken the claw.

Two aliens were deciding where to go on holiday. When they looked at the reviews for our Solar System, they decided not to come – we only have one star.

Why did the astronaut love going to space?

She thought it was out of this world.

Why couldn't the planet call up its friends?

It had Saturn its phone.

How do woolly pirates sail around?

On a pirate sheep.

What do you call a lost werewolf?

A where-wolf.

How do trains eat their lunch?

They chew chew.

Why was the broom running late?

It had overswept.

What do you call a robber in the Arctic?

A brrrrrrr-glar.

What's the largest moth in history?

The mammoth.

How do mountains keep warm?

They wear snow caps.

What do you call a snake that loves to build?

A boa constructor.

What did the snake have for lunch?

A ssssss-andwich.

What did the traffic light say to the other traffic light?

Why didn't the teddy bear eat its lunch?

Because it was stuffed.

Which is the most musical planet?

Nep-tune.

What did the ant say when it had a ride on the antelope's back?

'Wheeeeee!'

What did the duck say to the little ducks at the end of lunch break?

'Time to get quack to class.'

Did you hear about the frog who parked in the wrong place?

Its car got toad.

What's a frog's favourite outfit?

A jumpsuit.

What's a kangaroo's favourite snack?

Hop-corn.

What did the Stegosaurus use to chop up its wood?

A dino-saw.

What makes more noise than a T. rex?

Five T. rexes.

**What do you call
a dinosaur at Halloween?**

A Scareosaurus.

What's a sheep's favourite fruit?

A baaaa-nana.

What do you call a sheep covered in chocolate?

A chocolate baaaa.

What's a banana's favourite move in gymnastics?

The splits.

What did the lime say to the lemon?

'Sour you today?'

What did the lemon say to the lime?

'You're my zest friend.'

What do farts play in an orchestra?

Wind instruments.

Why do farts make bad spies?

They always blow their cover.

A man kept being late for work so he went to the shop and bought a giant alarm clock. When he went to bed that night, he lay down on top of the clock. He knew that he'd definitely wake up on time!

Did you hear about the woman who takes naps on a lamp?

She's a light sleeper.

What do gorillas use to wrap their presents?

Sticky ape.

What animal is always getting wet?

A rain-deer.

What type of dog loves a bath the most?

A shampoodle.

Where do snowmen book their holidays?

On the winter-net.

What did the snowman say to the icicle?

'I think you're really cool.'

Why are goalkeepers always so rich?

Because they are great at saving.

Did you hear about the angry cat?

She was furry-ous.

How do fleas prefer to travel?

By itch-hiking.

Did you hear about the man who got a job as a tailor?

It suited him very well.

What's a chicken's favourite book?

A hen-cyclopedia.

How many eggs does it take to build a house?

None – eggs don't have hands.

What did the boy say when he got his fifth cold of the year?

'Snot again.'

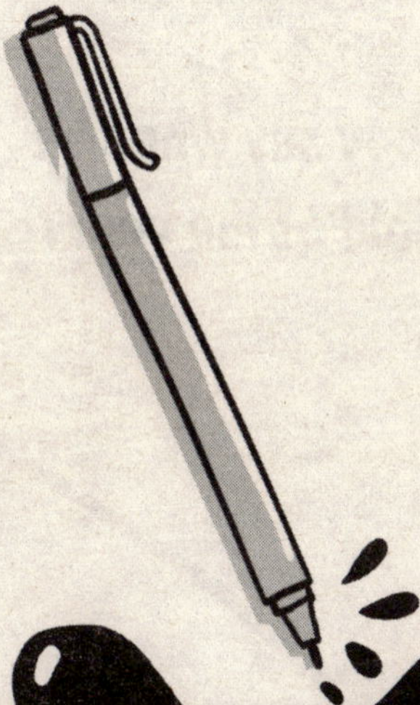

What did the pen say to its friend?

'You're ink-credible.'

Why do fish swim in big groups?

Because they can't walk.

What did the fish prince give Cinderella?

A glass flipper.

Knock, knock.

Who's there?

Fish.

Fish who?

Fish you'd stop knocking on my door.

Knock, knock.

Who's there?

Oil.

Oil who?

Oil be back tomorrow.

Why did the koala keep eating eucalyptus?

He couldn't leaf it alone.

Why do pandas never wear shoes?

Because they always have bear feet.

Why were the words best friends?

They were always on the same page.

Look out for other books in the series!

AMAZING JOKES FOR EVERY 6 YEAR OLD
What's noisier than a dinosaur?
Two dinosaurs!

AMAZING JOKES FOR EVERY 7 YEAR OLD
Where do frogs hang their coats?
In the croak-room.

AMAZING JOKES FOR EVERY 8 YEAR OLD

AMAZING GROSS FACTS EVERY 6 YEAR OLD NEEDS TO KNOW

AMAZING GROSS FACTS EVERY 7 YEAR OLD NEEDS TO KNOW

AMAZING GROSS FACTS EVERY 8 YEAR OLD NEEDS TO KNOW

AMAZING GROSS FACTS EVERY 9 YEAR OLD NEEDS TO KNOW

AMAZING GROSS FACTS EVERY 10 YEAR OLD NEEDS TO KNOW

AMAZING PUZZLES & QUIZZES FOR EVERY 6 YEAR OLD

AMAZING PUZZLES & QUIZZES FOR EVERY 7 YEAR OLD

AMAZING PUZZLES & QUIZZES FOR EVERY 8 YEAR OLD

AMAZING PUZZLES & QUIZZES FOR EVERY 9 YEAR OLD

AMAZING PUZZLES & QUIZZES FOR EVERY 10 YEAR OLD

AMAZING PUZZLES & QUIZZES HALLOWEEN

AMAZING PUZZLES & QUIZZES CHRISTMAS